Look out for other books in this series:

Charlie
& The Cat Flap

Charlie
& The Great Escape

Charlie
& The Big Snow

Charlie
& The Rocket Boy

Charlie
& The Cheese & Onion Crisps

www.hilarymckay.co.uk

Charlie
& The Haunted Tent

Hilary McKay
Illustrated by Sam Hearn

SCHOLASTIC

First published in the UK in 2008
by Scholastic Children's Books
An imprint of Scholastic Ltd
Euston House, 24 Eversholt Street
London, NW1 1DB, UK
Registered office: Westfield Road, Southam, Warwickshire, CV47 0RA
SCHOLASTIC and associated logos are trademarks and/or
registered trademarks of Scholastic Inc.

Text copyright © Hilary McKay, 2008
Illustrations © Sam Hearn, 2008
The right of Hilary McKay to be identified as the author of this work and of
Sam Hearn to be identified as the illustrator of this work has been asserted by them.
Cover illustration © Sam Hearn, 2008

ISBN 978 1407 10381 5

British Library Cataloguing-in-Publication Data
A CIP catalogue record for this book is available from the British Library

Printed by CPI Bookmarque, Croydon
Papers used by Scholastic Children's Books are made
from wood grown in sustainable forests.

1 3 5 7 9 10 8 6 4 2

www.scholastic.co.uk/zone

ONE

What happened in the morning

Charlie was seven years old and he lived with his father and mother and big brother Max.

"I am the normal one in the family," Charlie used to say. "Dad is old. Mum is dopey. Max thinks he's Superman or something!

Thank goodness for me!"

Max used to laugh when Charlie said that.

Max was not a bit like Charlie...

Max was tall and brainy and good at sports. He could ride a bike with no hands and do maths in his head.

"That's weird," said Henry, Charlie's best friend, who could not do maths anywhere, not in a maths books or on a calculator or even on his fingers.

Max knew which rock bands were good and which were rubbish. He could deal with spider invasions, and do somersaults on a trampoline and land the right way up.

"Showing off," said Henry, whose trampoline it was.

"What I don't understand," said Charlie, "is how he keeps his jeans up when he jumps so high."

"They can't be ordinary jeans," said Henry, "and his trainers can't be ordinary trainers either."

It was true that Max's trainers never flew off when he kicked a ball. And he never had to have jokes explained to him. And fizzy drinks did not come exploding out of his nose when he laughed.

"I'm glad he does not live with me!" said Henry.

Max went to Big School, which was not a bit like the school Charlie had to go to. Big School sounded like a sort of merry heaven, with its skiddy corridors and chewing gum dappled desks and handy sweetshop right next door. Max loved it, and every morning he got up early to catch the Big School bus.

Max was very, very aggravating early in the morning.

He did not give Charlie one second of peace.

One Friday he was even worse than usual.

"Buzz out of the way!" he ordered, rushing around completely dressed while Charlie was still half asleep in pyjamas and not even sure what day of the week it was.

"That's my toast! Give it back! Stand up a minute, you're sitting on my tie! Pass the cereal! Give me the TV remote! What are you watching that for?"

"It's my favourite," said Charlie.

"It's for toddlers!" said Max. "There's something in your hair, I think it might be jam. Leave my schoolbag alone, you can't borrow anything. What are you sucking? Is that from my packed lunch? When are you going to get dressed?"

"When are you going to stop bossing me about?" asked Charlie, yawning. "Can I have that orange juice?"

"No," said Max, "I just poured it out! Hey! Where are you taking it?"

But Charlie had gone, and so had the orange juice and the cocoa pops and the biscuit tin. He had decided it would be quieter to have breakfast in bed.

He had just got comfy when he heard Max calling from the front doorstep.

"Charlie!" shouted Max. "Charlie! Throw me down my football boots! Quick, before I miss the bus!"

"Growl, growl, growl," went Charlie.

"*Charlie!*" yelled Max. "*Boots!* Quick!"

"Boss, boss, boss!" muttered Charlie, taking no notice.

Then their mother joined in from the bathroom where she had been having a shower.

"Charlie!" she called. "Can't you hear Max?"

"Charlie, MOVE IT!" bellowed Max from the street.

"If I come in there and find you've gone

back to bed..." called Charlie's mother
from the bathroom.

"It's not fair!" complained Charlie. "I
was ASLEEP!"

All the same he rolled out of bed.

"HURRY!" ordered Max from the street.

Charlie stamped across to Max's boots,
dragged open the window, and flung them
as hard as he could, one,
two, at Max's annoying,
bossy head.

"NO!" roared Max.

But it was too late. There was a

pop like a huge balloon bursting.

A crash.

And then the sound of tinkling glass.

"Crikey," said Max.

The man-round-the-corner had a lovely yellow sports car. He parked it on Max and Charlie's street because he thought it was safer there than on the main road.

The lovely yellow sports car now had two football boots somewhere inside it and a huge terrible hole in the windscreen.

Charlie had a sudden longing to be in a very safe place.

Max seemed to go silent with shock.

Charlie's mother was not silent. She came out of the bathroom just in time to hear the second boot. She went wild. She marched into the bedroom and dragged Charlie out of from under the bed and into the street to see exactly what he had done.

"Open your eyes!" she commanded, in a terrible voice when he refused to look.

Charlie unscrunched his eyes for a second, looked, and quickly glanced away.

"And what is the-man-round-the-corner going say about that?"

"I dunno," said Charlie, picking up two little bits of glass and fitting them neatly together like a jigsaw puzzle. "I s'pose he won't be pleased. But it's his fault really. Leaving it there where anything might land on it."

"*What?*" asked Charlie's mother, as if she could not believe her ears.

"But he probably won't think that."

"So what do you suggest?" asked Charlie's mother, not very calmly.

"I s'pose you'll have to say sorry and explain you didn't mean it to happen."

"*I'll have to say sorry?*"

"Or could you just pretend you hadn't noticed?" asked Charlie hopefully.

"No, Charlie," said Charlie's (now mad with rage) mother. "I could not pretend I had not noticed. And I will not have to say sorry either. YOU threw the boots through his windscreen! So YOU will have to say sorry."

"Me?"

"Yes," said Charlie's mother and she pointed dramatically up the street.

"NOW!"

"But," said Charlie, now very frightened, "the-man-round the-corner is AWFUL about his car."

"I know," said Charlie's mother. "Off you go."

"I think I've forgotten where he lives!"

"Charlie!" said Charlie's mother in a scary quiet voice. "I may lose my temper."

So Charlie, in his pyjamas, set off to tell the man-round-the-corner what had happened to his car. He didn't want to, but he had to, because his mum had gone bonkers.

But he did not have to go on his own. Almost as soon as he set off he heard footsteps behind him.

"I'll come with you," said Max.

" Max did not just come with him. When the front door of the house round the corner opened and the man with the yellow car stood staring on the doorstep and Charlie became completely speechless, Max did the talking.

"I'm very, very sorry," said Max. "But I'm afraid there's been a dreadful accident with your car."

"An accident?"

"Its windscreen is broken."

"Broken?"

"Yes, and there's glass all inside. I'm terribly sorry. And please would you mind coming round and unlocking it because I'm afraid my football boots are inside and I need them at school today."

"Are you trying to tell me," demanded the man-round-the-corner, "that YOUR football boots BROKE my windscreen?"

Max nodded, and looked at Charlie who

was staring at them both with round horrified eyes and only just managing not to cry.

"It was an accident, wasn't it Charlie?" said Max.

"DON'T TRY AND TELL ME YOUR LITTLE BROTHER HAD ANYTHING TO DO WITH IT!" now yelled the man-round-the-corner. "Because I can see perfectly well the poor little lad's still in his pyjamas! Now get off home! And tell your parents I'll be round as soon as I've spoken to my insurers. And you can just manage without your blessed football boots today and I hope you're ashamed of yourself!"

And then he turned back inside and slammed the door.

All this time Charlie had not been able to speak a word. He had not even been able to move.

"Come on Charlie," said Max, and put an arm round his shoulder and led him away.

Charlie came, still speechless. He stayed that way until they were safely home. And then he found his voice at last and said, "Max."

"What?" asked Max.

"Thank you."

"Oh," said Max. "It was nothing."

What happened in the afternoon

Max and Charlie were so late for school
that day they had to be driven there by
their (only very slightly calmer) mother.
Max was the first to be dropped off. Max
rushed into school as if he was missing
something wonderful but when it came to
Charlie's turn he did not hurry. He walked
very slowly, as if in a daze. His head was

full of Max, and the way Max had gone with him and explained so politely, and put up with being yelled at, and never once said a single thing to suggest that the football boots had been thrown through the car window by himself, Charlie, in a moment of early morning grumpiness.

Charlie longed to do something wonderful for Max, to pay him back.

"Write him a sorry poem," suggested Henry. Henry often wrote sorry poems himself when he was in trouble. His mother had quite a collection. In fact, only that morning he had given her a new one that began:

...*Sorry I broke the handle off the loo* and actually ended with a rhyme...

"I'm really good at them," he continued, "I've done loads. I'll start you off if you like. Begin:

...Sorry I let the man-round-the-corner think you broke his car windscreen...

and go on with whatever you can think of for an excuse."

Charlie sighed.

"All you have to do is find a word that rhymes with windscreen! Easy peasy!"

"It's not enough," said Charlie. No poem, he was quite sure, not even one that happened to contain a rhyme for windscreen, would be enough to show Max how grateful he was. What was needed, he thought, was something much more heroic.

Something superheroish.

Such as a rescue from under the noses of roaring tigers.

Or the watery deck of a sinking ship.

Or the crumbling brink of a mile high cliff.

Or quicksand (which was an easy place to rescue someone from, because you just swam towards them over the surface with a rope in your teeth).

Or an attack by swamp-living boa constrictors (you unwind them by the tail, Charlie told himself, it cannot be difficult, unless there is more than one).

And if there was more than one, thought Charlie, the simple thing would be to tie their tails together. Then they would constrict each other and while they are doing it, I would grab Max and drag him out of the swamp ... it wouldn't be a problem...

Nor would aliens, if aliens tried to abduct him. I would simply invade their spaceship and baffle them with stuff they had never seen before. Like Suzy the cat, and my Bart Simpson torch, and my Tamagotchi. And while they were trying to

work out what they were I would spot the escape hatch and untie Max's legs. And then we would run (I'd let him go first) past the Controllers and right through the spaceship and down the escape hatch ...

and Max would be saved...

By me.

And afterwards, dreamed Charlie, when everything was over and the aliens were gone (caught by the police and put in the zoo. I'd help with that too.) then, afterwards, Max would say, "Charlie," and I'd say, "What?" and he'd say, Max would say, "Thank you."

"Oh," I'd say (calmer than anyone, James Bond or anyone), "It was nothing."

Every single one of the daydreams that Charlie dreamed that day ended this way. They cheered him up tremendously; he felt almost as if he really had done those things. The next time Max was in trouble, he decided, he would be there at once, rushing to the rescue like the most heroic of heroes.

He could hardly wait.

Charlie bounced home feeling good. He felt
even better when he saw that the yellow
sports car had disappeared from outside his
house. Only the tiniest sparkle of broken
glass showed it had ever been there.

"It is being fixed," said his mother, "and
we are paying the Excess and do not ask
what that means because I am no mood to
explain the details of car insurance to a
seven-year-old. But please understand that
all hope of a bouncy castle birthday party
is now completely over."

She was in a flap, Charlie saw. A
packing flap. She was charging round the
house flinging things into bags.

"That's yours," she said. "No, don't
take anything out! That's Max's ... That's

mine ... Those are for Gran..."

"But what's happening?" asked Charlie (who for one wild moment had thought they were having to move out because of the rage of the man-round-the-corner).

"Gran," said his mum. "She's had a fall and I must go over for a night or two. Your father is working all weekend and I can't take you with me ... Next door are feeding Suzy..." (that was the cat) "...Henry's mum's having you..."

"Oh, brilliant..." began Charlie, and paused. Henry's house was very close indeed to the house belonging to the man-round-the corner.

"And Max," said Charlie's mother, "is going to Aunt Emma." Charlie lost his breath and nearly fell over.

Aunt Emma was not a real aunt. She much older than a real aunt. She was Gran's older sister. Also she was Max's godmother. She was quite nice ... but ... she lived in a haunted house.

Once, when Max was seven years old, he had been sent to stay there.

"Never, ever, ever again am I going to Aunt Emma's," said Max when he got back. "Not in a million years. Not for a million pounds."

Ever since then, when ghost stories were being told, Max had remembered his visit to Aunt Emma's house. It had become a sort of family legend to the boys, even though their parents always said, "Utter rubbish!"

"YOU CAN'T," said Charlie,

remembering all this. "YOU CAN'T SEND MAX TO AUNT EMMA!"

"I can't not send Max to Aunt Emma," said Charlie's mother. "She invited him when she rang up about Gran."

"Where is he now?" asked Charlie.

"I'm here!" said Max, appearing suddenly behind them. "And it's NOT fair. Why can't I go to Henry's with Charlie? Or next door with Suzy? Why didn't you tell me sooner? I could have arranged a sleepover with someone from school. Why can't I stay here, anyway?"

"All on your own?" asked his mother. "Of course you can't!"

"It would be a million times better than being at Aunt Emma's all on my own," said Max.

Then, just for a second, he looked

hopefully at Charlie.

Charlie did not see the look because at that moment a car drove past the window and without even knowing quite how it happened he found himself flat on the floor behind the sofa.

"Wrong car," said Max. "Completely different. Not even yellow."

"I just fell over," said Charlie, crawling out backwards.

"'Course you did." Max gave the bag his mother had packed for him a big, unhappy kick.

"I suddenly slipped. And then I thought I'd look behind the sofa while I was down there."

Max shrugged.

"I wasn't scared."

"Did I say you were?"

"If you knew..." began Charlie, and then paused.

"If I knew what?"

All the things I would have rescued you from today, thought Charlie. If you'd needed me to. Lions! Drowning! Aliens! Crumbling cliff edges! Snake infested swamps ... (they were the easiest)...

Once more the delicious dreamy feeling of braveness crept over Charlie, warming him like sunshine.

I've been getting him out of trouble all day! he thought, looking proudly at Max.

Max gave his bag one last kick and slumped miserably down on the sofa.

"*Aunt Emma's!*" he complained.

Then Charlie the dream hero became Charlie the real hero.

"I'll come with you," he said.

THREE

What happened in the evening

When Henry heard the news he was furious.

"But you were coming here!" he wailed. "And I'd just got Mum to say we could camp in the garden instead of sleeping in the house. *Why* are you going with Max?

To get away from the man-round-the-corner?"

"No!" said Charlie, and he thought, did James Bond ever have to answer such stupid questions?

Charlie's mother was equally useless. She said, "You'd better not be planning anything silly."

Imagine, thought Charlie, James Bond going off on one of his missions and having to put up with his mum saying he'd better not be planning anything silly.

Nobody treated him like a superhero, not even Max. Max told him his ghost story all over again as they drove to Aunt Emma's.

"You don't know what you're letting yourself in for," Max said.

"Yes I do," said Charlie. "You've told me

dozens of times. Sleeping on the sofa bed in the dining room..."

"It smells of dinners," said Max.

"...In a black dark room where the light switch is next to the door so you have get out of bed and grope about on the wall to find it."

"I've brought a torch," said Max. "But something about that house jinxes torches. I couldn't get one to work last time."

"You told me that before too," said Charlie. "And about the scratching noises

and the tapping sounds and the way the air goes suddenly cold..."

"It's the sort of ghost," said Max, "that *touches* you. It breathed on me, did I tell you that? And then I felt its fingers in my hair."

"It was Aunt Emma" groaned Mum, from the front seat. "I've told you and told you it was just Aunt Emma!"

"There was no one there," insisted Max.

"She probably simply popped in to see if you were warm enough and kiss you goodnight."

"IT WAS NOT AUNT EMMA!" Max growled. "Aunt Emma doesn't even do stuff like that."

This seemed to be true.

"Max!" exclaimed Aunt Emma as soon

as they arrived. "How nice to have you here again! Relax! I won't kiss you! I remember how much I hated kissing relations when I was your age! And this is..."

"Charlie," said Charlie, giving her a very James Bond-ish look. "The name's Charlie."

"Charlie!" said Aunt Emma, looking down at him. "Goodness, how you've grown! Much more than Max has! Come in, 007!"

From that moment Charlie and Aunt Emma were friends. She was unlike anyone he had ever met before. She seemed to understand him. Right from the start, she treated him as if he was the bravest of the brave.

Because of this, Charlie became fearless.

When Aunt Emma sent him off with
Max to explore the house it was Charlie
who crawled among the boots and shoes in
the darkness of the cupboard under the
stairs.

"Why?" asked Max.

"Just checking for
skeletons," said
Charlie, airily.

At supper time it
was Charlie (who
was never allowed near the cooker
at home) who fried the sausages
and onions for hot dogs while
Max made banana splits for
pudding. The banana splits
were good, but Charlie's hot

dogs, nearly black and piled with onions, were fantastic.

Afterwards he astonished Max and Aunt Emma by scrubbing the frying pan clean.

"I thought it was beyond all help," said Aunt Emma. "I was going to throw it away!"

As a reward for cleaning the frying pan, Charlie was sent to climb a wobbly stack of chairs to the attic trapdoor in order to bring down a very smelly old tent.

"You won't want to use it tonight," said Aunt Emma as she helped them put it up in the garden (Max holding up poles while Charlie bashed in tent pegs with an enormous mallet). "It's far too musty. But by tomorrow it will be aired. You can sleep in it then if you like."

After the tent was up they went for a
run down to the park, before it was dark.
Max showed Aunt Emma football tricks
and Charlie showed her how he could hang
from his knees on the climbing frame. A
little while later he also showed her how

he could land from that position on to his head without making a fuss.

"I meant to do it," he said, when he had stopped blinking.

"We'll go home," said Aunt Emma, magnificently, "past the Hell's Angels Pub. You can have a drink and pick which motorbike you like best. The bikers line them up outside. They look wonderful."

The bikes did look wonderful. Max said he might start saving up. Charlie, swigging lemonade beside a crowd of leathery bikers, as close as he could get to the biggest bike of all, felt like he owned the lot all ready.

"Climb on if you like," said one bike's owner kindly.

"Wow!" said Charlie and vaulted on to the saddle as if he had done it all his life.

He stayed there until a yellow car drove up, causing him to tumble to the ground, dodge behind Max and Aunt Emma, and start running very fast.

"Race you back home," he called to Max, over his shoulder.

"It was a *completely* different car," Max yelled after him, and Charlie slowed down to a more dignified trot. He was quite recovered by the time Max and Aunt Emma caught up with him. They found him peering through the window of the dim shadowy dining room, in the hope of spotting a ghost.

Max bent down and peered too.

"You'll both be much too tired to be haunted," said Aunt Emma, laughing at them. "I hope you won't feel very disappointed if no ghosts turn up tonight."

"Charlie will be," said Max, and Charlie was.

ƒOUR

What happened in the dining room

Charlie was terribly disappointed.

He could hardly believe it. There they were, Charlie the hero and Max the terrified, side by side in their sleeping bags on Aunt Emma's pull-out sofa in the dinner-smelling dining room, all prepared and ready for the ghost.

And what had happened?

Not only was there no ghost, there was also no Max-the-terrified.

Max was fast asleep.

Asleep! thought Charlie. Snoring! And where *is* that beastly rotten spook?

Not here, growled Charlie to himself. After all that fuss! I could have been camping at Henry's!

The more he thought about this the more cross he became.

So cross, that when Max snored a particularly happy, comfortable snore, Charlie kicked him.

That was a good thing to do. It stopped the snoring at once. In a moment Max was awake and staring into the dark and asking (in a very panicky way), "What was that? What was that? Charlie, did you feel something?"

"It was only..." began Charlie, and then suddenly realized that his kick had been mistaken for a ghostly kick.

He had begun to say "it was only me" but now he changed his mind.

Charlie said, very calmly and soothingly, "I didn't feel anything. Go to sleep."

Max did, falling into sleep as quickly as he had tumbled awake.

Poor old Max, thought Charlie kindly, and gave him a little tiny poke.

And another, from the other side.

"Nooo!" moaned Max in his dreams and hid his head under his pillow.

He was clearly being haunted. Even his snoring sounded haunted.

There was something very pleasant, thought Charlie, about seeing brave Max hiding under a pillow.

But I'd better get him out, he decided after a while, in case he suffocates.

Very gently Charlie pulled the pillow away.

This woke Max. He rolled over, sat up, grabbed Charlie and shook him.

"Hello?" murmured Charlie, as if he had been asleep for hours.

"Charlie!" hissed Max urgently. "It's

here! I felt it in my sleep.
I went suddenly all cold.
Listen!"

Charlie listened
and heard the
sounds old houses
make at night; creaks
and rattles, bubbles in water pipes and the
wind in the trees outside. Nothing ghostly
at all, in fact he had never felt less
haunted in his life.

Max did not agree.

"It's just like last time," he said
unhappily.

"It's not like last time," said Charlie.
"Because I am here! I'll put the light on."
He hopped out of bed and groped his way
over to the switch by the door and flicked it.

Max sighed with relief.

"Doesn't it bother you?" he asked Charlie.

Charlie shook his head, smirking.

"Well, I hate it," said Max. "I knew it would be like this. It's just like before. I wish there was somewhere else we could go. I wish we could sleep in the tent ... Charlie!"

"What?"

"We *could* sleep in the tent! We've got sleeping bags! We can just get out the window!"

Charlie was not pleased. Any other time he would have loved to climb out of the window and sleep in a tent (especially when he was supposed to be sleeping somewhere else), but at the moment he was enjoying being the ghost that was haunting Max. He would have liked to do it for a bit longer.

"What if the tent is haunted too?" he asked.

"Don't be daft!" said Max, cheering up very quickly now that the light was on. "Whoever heard of a haunted tent? Hurry up!"

So Charlie hurried up. It was never much use arguing with Max when he had got an idea in his head. He knew that if he refused Max would go anyway and leave him behind in the dining room.

So he helped to very quietly open the dining room window and bundle the sleeping bags and pillows out into the garden. It was not long before they were back in bed again. This time the sounds were different, wind on canvas, the rustle of leaves, a tiny scuffling somewhere in the garden.

"That's better," said Max happily. "All right, Charlie?"

Charlie was not all right. His chance of being a hero had now completely gone. Max had rescued himself.

Bother oh bother oh bother, thought Charlie. Out loud he said, "Let's tell Awful Stories."

"In the morning," said Max, yawning.

"You don't really believe we left that ghost behind?"

"Yes I do," said Max. "Because you can tell when a place is haunted. You can tell by the horrible feeling you get. That dining room feels very, very haunted, but this tent is fine. Can't you tell?"

"They both feel exactly the same to me," said Charlie truthfully. "Anyway, what if the ghost gets out of the window?"

"I closed it," said Max, snuggling down in his sleeping bag.

Charlie suddenly remembered a useful ghostly fact.

"Ghosts can walk through walls!" he said. "So I

expect they can get out of windows dead easy! Dead! Ha! That's a joke. Dead! Get it?"

"Very, very funny," said Max sleepily.

"What I think is," said Charlie hopefully, "is that the ghost crept out of the window, and crawled after us across the lawn and is HERE RIGHT NOW!"

There was no reply.

Just a sleepy silence.

That went on.

And on.

And on.

Charlie gave a big sigh.

five

What happened in the tent

In the deepest, darkest part of the night
Charlie awoke with a thumping heart. It
was very quiet. Max lay motionless beside
him. All the same, Charlie knew some
noise had disturbed his dreams. Some alien
noise.

Charlie waited, listening in the darkness.
The cold was horrible. It came in icy

waves, lapping over his face.

"Max," whispered Charlie.

The air in the tent smelled of dampness and attics and old, old age. The cold grew worse. Outside something rattled and rattled. A strange shape moved on the canvas wall of the tent, a round darkness, like the tip of a finger, slowly tracing a small faint line.

WHAM!

Something enormous landed in the middle of Charlie's stomach.

"Max!" yelled Charlie. "It's here! It's come back! It must have really followed us out of the window!"

Max groaned.

"Get up! Get out! I know what to do!"

Even as he spoke Charlie was already outside the tent, and tugging Max, sleeping bag and all, on to the grass. "Out of the way!" he yelled, running round in the dark, pulling up tent pegs and unhooking guy ropes. "Mind the poles! Ha!"

The tent collapsed while Max, the snail who had left the ghostly trail on the canvas and next door's cat (who had only jumped on Charlie to see what he was) all stared in amazement.

"Ha!" shouted Charlie. "Got him! Got him, Max! Trapped! Squashed flat!"

"Charlie, you nutter!" said Max. "Now what'll we do?"

"Lie down on him!" cried Charlie. "Keep him squashed! Come on!"

He flung his sleeping bag on the heap of tent and wriggled inside it. Max, after a few moments hesitation, did the same.

"I bet he wasn't expecting that," said Charlie, smugly.

"I bet he wasn't," agreed Max.

"I should think it would put him off haunting for life. Well, not for life ... because of course he's dead, but you know what I mean ... put him off jumping on people, anyway."

"Is that what happened then? Did something jump on you?"

"Yep."

"What did it feel like?"

"Heavy. And strong. And enormous. Have you ever been jumped on by Henry?"

"Yes."

"Well, like that. Only bigger. Like about ten Henrys."

"Not like a cat?"

"No!"

"I just wondered, because there's a cat on the fence. I just wondered if it could have been that."

"No," said Charlie. "Ten million times bigger. Definitely. Don't worry though. It must be flattened by now."

Max chuckled.

The cat on the fence stuck a leg straight in the air and began a midnight bath. The snail that had hidden ever since his journey up the wall of the tent had been so surprisingly interrupted, once again began his travels. Aunt Emma's garden began to feel a very peaceful place.

"This is really good," said Max. "Look at the stars!"

"Stars are all right," said Charlie, "but they're not star shaped, are they? They shouldn't really be called stars I don't think."

"What'd you call them, then?"

Charlie paused, trying to think of a better name for stars than stars, and at that moment the snail met an enormous obstacle in his midnight trip across the canvas of the tent.

The obstacle was Charlie.

The snail was a stubborn snail. He did not give up or turn back. He began, very slowly, to climb over.

"I'd call stars..." began Charlie, "something more like ... WHAAAH!"

It felt just like a cool finger had reached over Charlie's pyjama top and touched his shoulder. "It's in my sleeping bag!" he bawled. "Crikey! Now my sleeping bag's haunted!"

He struggled out, rolled it up, jumped on it, fell on it, punched it and sat on it, panting. The snail clung, terrified, to the collar of his pyjamas. The cat disappeared over the far side of the fence.

"Has it gone?" asked Max, half dead with laughing.

"I think so," said Charlie, gripping his sleeping bag tight shut. "It's not in here anyway ... EEEUUYUK!"

"What now?"

"It licked my neck! *It's in my pyjamas*!"

"*Charlie!*" protested Max, but already parts of pyjamas were flying through the air.

"That's
disgusting!"
roared Charlie, "I'm
not putting up with it!
A ghost in my pyjamas
LICKING MY NECK!"

Bare and indignant Charlie
grabbed his pyjamas, screwed
them, knotted them and hurled
them in a ball over the fence.

"There!" he yelled.
"That's it! Gone! Hurray! I've got rid of it!
I did it! I did it! Did you see that, Max?"

"Yes. Yes I did," said Max. "You emptied
the ghost out of your sleeping bag and
screwed it up in your pyjamas and chucked
it over the fence. It was fantastic."

"I bet you're glad I came," said Charlie,
clambering back into his sleeping bag.

"Yes I am," said Max.

"Do you think it's worth trying to go to sleep?"

"Don't know. Might be."

Charlie sighed and burrowed into the folds of collapsed tent.

In the garden next door the cat sniffed his pyjamas and then curled up in the middle of them and closed his eyes.

However the snail, who had clung desperately to Charlie's pyjama collar as he flew over the fence, uncurled and hurried away.

Charlie went to sleep, and Max went to sleep, and the cat went to sleep, but the snail did not. He slid off and hid in the bushes and never went camping again.

What Henry thought

On Monday afternoon as Charlie and
Henry walked home from school Charlie
told Henry all about Aunt Emma's and
the haunted tent and the battle under the
stars that he had fought to save Max from
the ghost.

Henry said, "It doesn't sound much like
you."

Charlie admitted he supposed it didn't.

"And are you sure you can actually collapse a tent on a ghost and shake it out of a sleeping bag and squash it flat and throw it over a fence?" asked Henry. "Because I've never heard of anyone doing it before."

"Ask Max if you don't believe me," said Charlie, crossly.

"It didn't come back then?"

"No. Not that night, nor the next night when we had to sleep in the dining room because it rained so much water poured in through the holes in the tent. It didn't come back at all."

"Perhaps the rain put it off."

"I put it off!" said Charlie.

"Oh yes, of course," said Henry politely. "Do you remember when there were ghosts on Doctor Who and you hid behind the sofa with your fingers in your ears?"

Charlie, stooping to pick up a penny from the gutter, wished very hard that a ghost would swoop up right at that moment and get Henry there, where he stood, in the middle of the street. He decided that if this happened he would not do a thing to prevent it.

"Have you started collecting pennies?" asked Henry. "Is it to help pay for the man-next-door's windscreen?"

Charlie decided he *would* help the ghost if it came. Out loud he said huffily, "I'm saving up for a motorbike."

"That'll be nice," said Henry. "As long as it doesn't go too fast. Like the Thomas the Tank Engine roundabout in the marketplace that you had to have stopped because you were frightened."

Then he and Charlie glared at one another.

"You are horribler than you used to be," remarked Charlie.

"Me?" asked Henry. "*Me* horribler? Me who you wouldn't come and stay with? After I got my mum to say we could camp in our garden? You don't know what hard work that was! I had to pester until she nearly went *mad*! And then you went off to your rotten Aunt Emma's and had a brilliant time going to the pub and trying out motorbikes and scaring off ghosts (in your dreams) and now I don't suppose you ever will want to come camping in my garden. Not with the man-next-door whose windscreen you smashed living so close!"

Charlie was silent.

"I s'pose you're still scared of *him*!"

Charlie supposed he was too.

"Although I can't see why. It's Max he thinks did it, not you."

This was awful.

"Poor Max," said Henry.

Yes, poor Max! agreed Charlie, silently, and he thought, and poor me, too! What had happened since he got home again? he wondered. It had been so easy to be brave at Aunt Emma's house. Where had all the braveness gone? Would he never be a superhero again? Was he always going to be afraid of the man-round-the-corner, and would be man-round-the-corner always believe it was Max who smashed his windscreen?

Was there not, Charlie asked himself desperately, even a tiny bit of braveness left to remind him of how lovely it had been?

Charlie started to walk faster.

And then to jog.

And then he was running, sprinting, pounding down the road to the house of the man-round-the-corner, up the steps, hammering at the door.

"It was me!" he panted as soon as it
opened. "Me who broke your windscreen!
Not Max! Me!"

The man-round-the-corner was as rude
as ever. "You," he said. "Oh. Not the big
kid, the little kid. Well. Makes no
difference to me."

But it made a difference to Charlie.

A wonderful difference.

He flew past Henry, who was standing staring on the pavement, down the street, into his own house, and up the stairs.

Max was sitting at the table of the room they shared, staring at his homework.

"I did it Max!" Charlie shouted, "I told him. The man-round-the-corner! I went to his house and told him about breaking his windscreen! I said it wasn't you! I told him it was me!"

"You did?" asked Max, and now although he was still sitting at the table, staring at his homework, he was smiling the most enormous smile.

"Yes," said Charlie.

Then he turned and jumped back down the stairs again and rushed outside to find Henry and tell him he would come camping in his garden any time he liked.

"Let's go and start work on my mum right now!" said Henry joyfully.

They hurried off to begin at once, and it was such hard work and took so long that Charlie forgot all about the man-round-the-corner.

He didn't think of him once until bedtime, when Max said suddenly, "Charlie."

"What?" asked Charlie.

"Thanks."

"Oh," said Charlie. "It was nothing."

Meet Charlie – he's trouble!

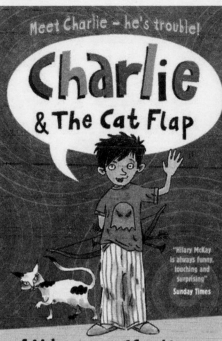

Meet Charlie – he's trouble!

Charlie & The Cat Flap

"Hilary McKay is always funny, touching and surprising"
Sunday Times

Hilary McKay

Charlie and Henry are staying the
night at Charlie's house. They've made
a deal, but the night doesn't go quite
as Charlie plans. . .

Meet Charlie – he's trouble!

Charlie's fed up with his mean family always picking on him – so he's decided to run away. That'll show them! Now they'll be sorry!

But running away means being boringly, IMPOSSIBLY quiet…

Meet Charlie - he's trouble!

"The snow's all getting wasted! What'll we do? It will never last till after school!"

Charlie's been waiting for snow his whole life, but now it's come, everyone's trying to spoil it! Luckily, Charlie has a very clever plan to keep it safe...

Meet Charlie - he's trouble!

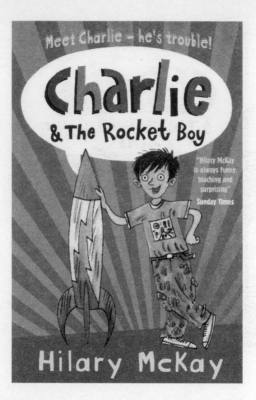

*"Zachary is a liar, liar,
pants on fire!"*

There's a new boy in Charlie's class. Zachary says his dad is away on a rocket but Charlie knows that's rubbish ... Isn't it?

Meet Charlie – he's trouble!

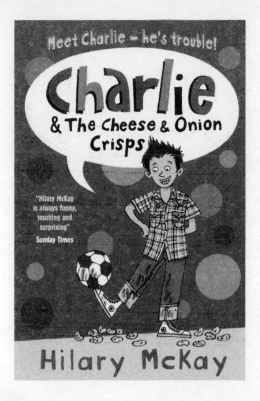

*Charlie has given up
cheese and onion crisps!*

He just hasn't been himself lately.
There's only one thing for it - the Truly
Amazing Smarties Trick!